In dedication to
Gordon Woodgate

This paperback edition first published in 2022 by Andersen Press Ltd.

First published in Great Britain in 2021 by Andersen Press Ltd.,

20 Vauxhall Bridge Road, London, SW1V 2SA, UK

Vijverlaan 48, 3062 HL Rotterdam, Nederland

Copyright © Harry Woodgate, 2021.

The right of Harry Woodgate to be identified as the author and

illustrator of this work has been asserted by them in accordance

with the Copyright, Designs and Patents Act, 1988.

Printed and bound in Spain.

British Library Cataloguing in Publication Data available.

ISBN 978 1 78344 992 7

Grandad's Camper

Harry Woodgate

ANDERSEN PRESS

Every summer I go to stay at my grandad's house
by the sea. It's a pretty, old cottage,

with bookshelves packed to the brim with
interesting things from Grandad's travels,

and lots of brilliant places to play hide and seek!

In the garden, Grandad grows
all kinds of fruit and vegetables.

**The item should be returned or renewed
by the last date stamped below.**

Dylid dychwelyd neu adnewyddu'r eitem erbyn
y dyddiad olaf sydd wedi'i stampio isod.

Newport
CITY COUNCIL
CYNGOR DINAS
Casnewydd

PILLGWENLLY

To renew visit / Adnewyddwch ar
www.newport.gov.uk/libraries

There's a big cherry tree,
which if you shake just
enough... Yum!

But my favourite thing to do at Grandad's house is snuggle up on the sofa and listen as Grandad tells me about all of the amazing places he and Gramps would explore.

"Your Gramps was quite the adventurer!

He was tall and handsome,

and excellent at so many things…

tidiness was not one of them!

Soon after we met he invited me on holiday

so we set off in his camper to the seaside.

In the daytime we surfed,

ate fish and chips,

and we had a sandcastle competition...

... I think I won!

Then in the evenings
we'd have bonfires
on the beach

and watch the tide
going in and out
of the bay.

One afternoon,
Gramps said to me, 'There
are so many wonderful things
in this world, and I want to
see them all with you.'
So that's exactly what we did.

Gramps always wanted
to visit the city, so that's
where we went first.

We drove through dark tunnels, over fancy bridges,

and in between towering skyscrapers.

Everywhere was full
of life – there were
so many people,

so many animals,
and so many things
to see.

It was amazing.

We saw lots of different kinds of homes,

from high-rise flats

to terraces and town houses.

But we were happy with our little home on wheels, which we could take wherever we pleased."

Grandad puts down his photo album and smiles. I can see how much he loves those memories and how much he loved Gramps.

"Why don't you go anywhere now, Grandad?"

"It's not the same without Gramps – he made everything feel extra special. Now he isn't around, I just don't feel like it."

A thought pops into my head. "Do you still have your camper van?" He winks. "Follow me!"

I run outside to
the garage and with all
my might, heave open the big old doors…

There it is! It looks rather
sorry for itself, but I come
up with a clever plan.

"Let's fix it up and go to
the seaside. Together!"
He looks at me and laughs.
"I suppose we can take
one more trip."

So off comes the dust
sheet and we get to
work.

Finally we stand
back and look at
our handiwork.

"Your Gramps would be so happy to see this. It's what he would have wanted. I think we should pack some snacks and hot chocolate and we can go and camp on the beach – just like we used to!"

So that's exactly what we do.